# Table of Contents

# Claimed By Fallon
## (Mountain Man Romance)
### By Mel Pate

# Copyright page

# Chapter 1

Dakota

My feet are aching as I reach for the coffeepot, refilling Fred's coffee cup. Cheryl comes walking towards the counter I'm standing behind with a grin, slapping a number down on the counter. "That's three this week," she says with a broad grin.

I shake my head and laugh at her. "You only have two nights off a week. What are you doing taking a third number?"

She shrugs, walking past. "It's a backup in case one of the others cancels."

Cheryl is beautiful, with long blonde hair and an hourglass figure. But she's as wild as they come. Since there's nothing to do in North Ridge, she makes it a point to have a man lined up for her nights off at the diner for 'her entertainment.'

"What are you going to do when two show up here or at your place and discover you are dating more than one?" Fred asks her with a smirk.

Fred is in his 60s and owns the hardware store. He's by far my favorite regular in the diner. Fred's funny and likes to work the crossword puzzles while chatting with us waitresses until we close each night. He's lonely. I know that feeling all too well.

Cheryl swings around and flashes Fred a million-dollar smile with a raised brow. "Make it a party instead of a date."

Poor Fred's eyes go wide, and I burst with laughter, walking over to top off Doug's coffee. The local barber may pretend not to hear the conversation, but I know he doesn't miss anything. In his line of work, I doubt there's anything he doesn't know about the residents.

"In my day, a woman found a good man and settled down, had a family," Fred says over his coffee cup. But I don't miss his grin.

Cheryl places both palms on the counter and tilts her head in contemplation. "Fred, if there was an ice cream shop here, would you taste the different flavors?"

He cocks a brow. "Sure."

She nods with a broad smile. "That's what I'm doing. Sampling what's on the menu."

I nearly choke on air when I see his stunned expression. If she was going for the shock factor, she nailed it.

She stopped, tossing me a look over her shoulder, analyzing me for a minute. "If you'd say yes to the customers once in a while instead of being all proper, you'd be more fun to work with."

I look down at my T-shirt, blue jeans, and tennis shoes. I'm a waitress who's tired, nearing the end of her shift. Tendrils of hair have worked their way out of my ponytail, with spots of who knows what kinds of food on my apron. Proper doesn't describe me.

I look back at her cleaning off a table and shake my head, setting the coffeepot back in its spot to start cleaning up with her.

"I wasn't talking about your clothes, you know," she says as I begin refilling the sugar, salt, and pepper on each table. "This isn't the 1950s. Women own their sexuality now."

I screw the lid back on the container I just filled, sitting it back in place. "Cheryl, if having fun with the truckers that come through here makes you happy, go for it. That's just not me. I'm just worried that one day it will blow up on you when they all find out."

I hear her heave a sigh, but she doesn't reply.

The diner doesn't get any more customers after 8, so we'll be ready to close up once the clock reaches 9. Lucy comes out of the kitchen looking tired. "Go home. I'll finish up tonight."

She gives me an appreciative smile. Lucy and Tom, our cook, own the diner, and most days, they're here open to close. At their age, I know it's hard on them.

"I don't want to leave you alone," she says, but I see the weariness in her eyes.

"It's only 30 more minutes, and everything's done. Go on." I pat her shoulder with a sad smile.

"I'm used to it." It's the truth. Since I was 16, it's just been me. Although since I moved here 6 months ago, Lucy and Tom have treated me like family.

"Go home and rest. That man of yours will be home shortly," I say with a grin.

Lucy smiles, looking towards the kitchen. I've never seen two people more in love. Even after all the years they've been married, you would think they were newlyweds the way they look at each other.

I want that. Maybe one day, my inner voice says.

"See you tomorrow," she says, yawning, walking back to the kitchen. No doubt to kiss Tom before leaving out the back.

I refill Fred's coffee cup since he's the last one here and begin wiping down the counter again. I want a man in my life, but the ones that come through here. I shake myself at the thought.

Plenty of travelers and truckers have hit on me. They want in my jeans, but that's not happening. Tom had to let some of the regulars passing through know that I was off the menu and that they had better not touch me again without consent, or he'd have to deal with them. None of them have smacked my butt or touched me since.

I'm not interested in just jumping into bed with someone, and certainly not for my first time. However, being attracted to strong alpha types presents a problem. Most of them are assholes. The sweet ones never interest me.

Too bad I haven't met anyone who's caught my interest since moving here.

"I'm closing the kitchen," Tom calls out through the window to the kitchen.

"Ok," I say, glancing at the clock, seeing it's 15 minutes until closing.

"A six-letter word for fragments ends in 's,'" Fred says, staring at his crossword book.

I think for a minute before grinning. "Pieces."

His head snaps up with a smile. "Smart and pretty. Too bad I'm not 40 years younger."

I laugh and shake my head. He's a sweetheart. But we both know that no one will ever compare to his wife. He's just lonely since she passed.

I do appreciate his company every night when things get quiet.

I'm about to go to the bathroom when the roar of an engine gets my attention. It's not the sound of a semi coming from the lumberyard or gravel pit. It's a rumbling V-8, and it's moving fast.

We both turn towards the glass windows, watching the road, when a pickup comes screeching into the parking lot. The lift kit and tires have it so high up it looks like a monster truck.

The hairs on the back of my neck stand on end, and I know that something bad's about to happen.

Fred stands and points towards the kitchen. "Get in the back, tell Tom the Brady brothers are out of prison and are here."

Prison. Brothers. Trouble. The words repeat in my head before I can get my feet moving.

Fred goes for the door, no doubt to lock it since he's closer, and I charge into the kitchen, the swinging door slamming against the wall.

Tom turns away from the grill he was cleaning wide-eyed. There's shouting, and a single shot fired, making my eyes water. Is Fred ok?

"What?" Tom says, taking steps toward me and the door to the front of the diner.

I rush forward, fear gripping me. "Brady brothers, prison here," I blurt out in a rush.

Tom's eyes go wide before simultaneously shoving me behind him and grabbing a huge chef's knife off the rack.

I follow him out, needing to know if Fred is okay, but we don't make it through the door. A huge man burst through the swinging door with an evil grin. "Where's the rest of the money?"

My eyes go past him, seeing a busted cash register on the floor, but what makes my chest clench is seeing Fred on the floor and a man kicking him even though he looks to be unconscious.

"Stop!" I scream so loud my throat feels like it tore, and tears stream down my face. I try to go around Tom to get to poor Fred, but Tom shoves me back behind him.

Both of these men look evil and not above killing to get whatever they want. The one in front of us starts laughing at hearing his brother trash the front of the diner. I feel relief that he's now leaving Fred alone. Maybe he'll be ok if we can keep them away from him. His face is bloody, and I'm scared that they may have already killed him.

A chair gets thrown past the door, and I hear glass shatter, but none of that matters. They need to leave.

"The money, old man," the evil Brady brother demands, stepping closer to us.

Tom holds the knife up, never faltering, ready to take him on. Which is stupid because he's holding a gun. A knife against a gun will lose every time.

I glance around, looking for something to pick up to use as a weapon if I need to, but nothing's within reach. My heart is pounding so hard that my chest hurts, and my vision is blurry from tears.

"Get the hell out of my diner," Tom demands, gripping the knife tighter in his large hand. "Or I swear I'll gut you."

The man laughs, and it's so evil a chill goes down my spine. He takes a step forward, and Tom swings the knife right at his face, but the Brady brother catches his forearm in one hand before he punches Tom so hard his head snaps back.

Blood gushes from Tom's nose, and the knife falls to the floor, skating across it towards the stove.

I release my grip on the back of Tom's shirt and dive for it.

Just as I'm about to wrap my fingers around it, pain explodes in the side of my face, knocking me into the stove.

My vision fades, and all the air in my lungs rushes out. With shaky hands, I clutch both sides of my head, trying to force myself not to scream.

I've been hit before, but never that hard. I'm scared, pissed off, and I know we have to make it out of this alive. Crying won't solve anything but give them more power.

I open my eyes and reach for the knife again, but I'm picked up by my hair and tossed across the kitchen, my back hitting the fridge.

Pain explodes through me, and this time, a scream escapes.

Through tear-filled eyes, I see both brothers jump on Tom, punching him until he falls, and then they begin to kick him. "NO!" I scream, jumping to my feet before diving on top of him to offer some protection. I can't fight both these men, but I can protect Tom from the blows.

I stiffen, waiting for the hits and kicks to rain down on me, but I feel nothing.

Someone from the front of the diner yells, they gotta go.

I hear boots hitting the floor in determined steps, so I climb off Tom, seeing his blood-covered face. When the bell chimes, I know they're gone, but the damage is done.

"Are you ok?" I ask, taking his hand to help him sit if he can.

Tom gets to a sitting position, leaning against the walk-in freezer.

My whole body is shaking, from adrenaline, fear, both.

He cups his nose, that's clearly broken, before spitting out a mouth full of blood onto the floor. "Not the first time it's been broken. Probably won't be the last."

"Fred," I breathe out, jumping to my feet and running towards the front. The diner's destroyed, including two large windows. My chest clenches at the sight. This is the first place that's felt like home to me.

I drop to my knees beside Fred, cradling his head in my hands. His eyes open, and he takes a minute to focus on me. Then he abruptly sits up, jerking me into a bone-crushing hug. "We're ok. They're gone. It's over." I hug him back, just as fiercely, needing something to cling onto.

He leans back and looks at the doorway to the kitchen where Tom is standing. I've never seen Tom pissed until now. The dark look in his eyes holds a promise of retribution and pain. "It isn't over. It's just begun."

His voice is so low, deep, and dangerous a shiver goes up my spine.

"Damn straight," Fred says, getting to his feet, then reaching out a hand to help me up.

All I can think, looking between them, is there's more to these two men than I realized. And after what the Brady brothers did, I won't feel sorry for whatever they have planned for them.

# Chapter 2

Dakota

Getting out of my car the next morning, I see Tom, Lucy, and Cheryl all standing at the door, waiting for Tom to unlock it. I wanted to stay with them last night while they got supplies from the hardware store to board up the broken windows, but they refused, saying I needed rest after everything that happened.

I approach them as the door opens, seeing the tears in Lucy's eyes. This diner was her and Tom's dream, and they built it up over the years. To see this must be breaking her heart. "Dear lord," she gasps, covering her mouth.

"This is fucked," Cheryl says with her mouth agape. "What happened?"

I follow everyone inside, and broken glass crunches beneath our feet with every footstep. Tables and chairs are overturned, and the cash register on the floor is busted to pieces like a hammer was taken to it. Everything that was on the counter is now on the floor, broken. I glance at the back wall and see both coffee machines intact.

Well, at least I can put coffee on before we start tackling the mess.

"The Brady brothers were released from prison and paid us a visit," Tom says with a snarl.

Lucy doesn't look surprised, I'm sure, hearing the details from Tom last night when he arrived home.

Cheryl, however, jerks her head to Tom with a look of shock so fast I'm surprised she doesn't have whiplash. "What?"

I put my purse under the counter and washed my hands to make coffee. By the time Tom told her everything that had happened last night, she was in tears.

Once I finish getting both pots on to perk, I grab my purse and remove the makeup I purchased on my way in this morning. Leaving home at 16, I never learned how to put the stuff on, and I'm hoping Lucy will help me.

I palm the concealer, foundation, and powder the lady at the general store suggested and walk over to Lucy. For the first time, she takes in the side of my face.

My left eye is bruised, my temple, and part of my cheek. Her eyes start to fill with tears again, but I shake my head. "Don't. I'm fine. But can you help me?" I ask, holding up the three containers.

She looks at them and then takes them, gesturing for me to sit. "Of course, dear."

By the time the coffee's ready and we all have cups, she has my bruises covered well enough that I won't scare people off. Thankfully, she explained what she was doing so I could do it myself tomorrow.

The bell above the door chimes, and we all turn, seeing Fred and Doug come in. They both have hard expressions, looking around at the destruction.

I stand, heading for the broom and dustpan to get started on cleaning up while they talk.

"Tell me everything," Doug says in a firm tone, staring at Tom.

Tom's jaw flexes, and I go back to sweeping all the glass into piles so it's easier to clean up.

They finish the story by admitting that both he and Fred had to make a trip to the hospital an hour away. Tom's nose is set and taped up, definitely broken, and Fred's ribs are wrapped because they fractured three of them.

"It could have been worse," Fred admits, shaking his head.

"How are they out of prison?" Doug asks in disbelief. "They shot a man during a robbery, and 5 years is all they served?" His voice is raising with each word he bites out.

Oh crap, that got my attention. We were lucky then because the shot they fired here looked like it was a warning shot into the ceiling. This is my family now. I can't imagine any of them getting shot or, worse, killed.

They all sit except Lucy and me, who are busy trying to make a dent in cleaning up this mess.

"We can't let this slide, and the cops in Newton aren't going to do much except put out an 'All-Points Bulletin' on them. We're on our own here." Doug's face is hard and angry as he speaks.

"We're not letting them get away with this," Tom says, slamming his coffee cup down. "I called the Denton Brothers."

Cheryl comes to my side, examining my face. "Who is that?" I ask. Knowing I've heard their names before, but not remembering who they are.

"They really did a number on you," she says, reaching up to touch my temple.

I pull back because it's still tender to the touch. "I'm fine, really."

Lucy keeps glancing over to Tom as if making sure he's really here and ok. Jealousy for what they have shoots through me. I hope one day I have a man in my life to worry about. To love.

"I hope the Denton's give those fuckers what they deserve," she says, dropping her hand and stepping back.

Well, if she's this angry looking at my face, I guess the makeup doesn't hide everything. I haven't looked in the mirror since Lucy put it on for me.

I continue sweeping, listening to conversations around me. Why didn't Cheryl answer my question? I wonder.

"Dakota, are you ok?" Tom's deep voice startles me for a minute and I turn.

Fred and Doug are now staring at me, too, and I feel uncomfortable with all eyes on me. "I'm fine, Tom. I only got hit once," I say, looking between him and Fred. "You two got it much worse."

I don't mention getting thrown and the bruise on my back.

He nods but clenches his hand into a fist on the table. "Just know that they'll get what's coming. No one touches my family and just walks away."

There is a deadly tone to his voice, and I believe every word.

"They didn't just hit here. They broke into the barbershop, too," Doug says. "Like barber shops have a bunch of cash on hand." He shakes his head, and I almost laugh at how stupid the Brady brothers are. But I don't. Nothing about any of this is funny.

Lucy jumps when Tom slams his fist onto the table, and the sugar container crashes to the floor.

"Damn it!" Tom yells. "They'll pay for everything they've done."

Lucy and Cheryl exchange worried glances before looking at me. I wish they would explain what they're thinking.

"We need to stay armed and on the lookout until they're taken care of," Tom says, and Fred and Doug both agree.

The room goes quiet except for the sounds of us sweeping up glass and the occasional sound of Lucy righting chairs and tables to their correct place.

Cheryl and I keep exchanging looks, wondering what's going to happen.

"When are Fallon and Duke going to be here?" Fred finally asks Tom.

That's it, I think. The Denton brothers are Fallon and Duke, and I knew I'd heard them mentioned before.

The Dentons are the family that lives up on the mountain and rarely comes down since their parents passed away. They stay up there with their sister, only coming down once a month for supplies or to check in on the lumber mill and gravel pit. The two businesses the family owns.

Everyone is very quiet about them except to say they keep to themselves.

Cheryl's eyes widen, and her mouth drops open, staring at me.

"What?" I whisper.

"You'll see when they get here," she says with a grin, then looks down at her clothes.

Hmm, by the way, she's acting, they must be good-looking. But from the way the men are talking, they also sound dangerous.

"I wish I had been here," Doug says, and we all turn to look at him.

"What would you have done? They were armed. We weren't," Tom says, pausing, then looking at me. "I think you surprised them, though."

My eyebrows shoot up into my hairline at that. "How?" All I did was scream for them to stop.

Tom shakes his head before looking me dead in the eye. "You didn't cower in fear like most would. And you tried protecting us. By the looks on their faces, you shocked them."

I feel the heat rising to my cheeks. I didn't plan or think at all while it was happening. My survival instincts took over. I just wanted them to leave.

With no retort, I continue sweeping the mess into piles as best I can until anger rises.

This is not just my place of work. These people helped me with a job when I needed it, find an apartment, even brought me soup and took care of me when I was sick. They're my family. For this to happen to them has my temper flaring.

If the Denton brothers don't do something about this, I may have to devise something crazy. No way the Brady's get away with this.

# Chapter 3

Dakota

I approach Fred, who's leaning against the counter next to the window. He's clutching his side, revealing the pain he feels from his broken ribs. "Why aren't you at home taking it easy?"

He shifts his gaze to me with an easy smile and soft eyes. "I'm right where I need to be. We all need to be alert until things are handled." His eyes drift to the shotgun leaning against the glass just inches in front of him before he looks back out the window.

Whenever he hears a vehicle, his head whips in the direction it's coming from, as if he's on sentry duty guarding us all.

"You want a refill?" I ask, pointing to his coffee cup.

"Sure," he replies while constantly scanning the area outside.

I take the pot of steaming coffee to top him off, but a question lingers in the back of my mind: "Do you think they'll come back?"

"Doubt it. They'll know we'll be prepared." His tone is almost dismissive.

"Then what are you watching for?" I ask, leaning my elbows on the counter.

"Fallon and Duke will be here soon. They'll want to see the damage and talk to everyone involved." His eyes flick to me before returning his gaze back outside.

Dang, it's like everyone in town looks up to these guys as if they're a force to be reckoned with. A part of me looks forward to meeting them. "You respect them," I say without thinking. Sometimes, my mouth has a mind of its own.

He side-eyes me with a look I don't recognize. "Their grandparents founded this town. Any problems that arise, they handle it. Always have." He pauses, taking a drink of coffee. "You don't mess with anything under their protection without consequence."

I follow his movements when he sits his cup down and continues staring outside. His words bouncing around in my head. They sound both dangerous and protective. Now I'm not sure what I think about meeting them.

I stand straight, looking around at the piles of glass, knowing I need to finish cleaning it up. Gloves, I think as I eye the large pieces that I know won't sweep up in a dustpan.

Before I could take a step to find some, Fred's words stopped me. He must have seen the look on my face, taking it for concern.

"Duke's the quiet one. He was called 'The Tank' when he was younger. If you messed with his family or someone he cared about, he would bulldoze you down without a word. Put a boy in double leg casts on the football field after breaking both legs for trying to mess with his sister before the game that night," he says, shaking his head, laughing. "As for Fallon...Some say he's crazy. But he just acts before thinking rationally. He's the oldest, but also the fiercest."

I swallow hard, staring at the side of his face. "So they protect their family?"

He turns, meeting my eyes, and one side of his mouth lifts in a half smile. "Family, the town, and everyone in it."

His words have my chest tightening. I've taken care of myself most of my life. Even as a child, I didn't truly have a childhood. I always look after myself. It must be nice knowing someone cares enough to be there for you that way. I envy their sister, feeling safe and cared for.

I shake my head, clearing those thoughts. It's crazy to feel jealous of someone you've never even met. Feeling things like that get you nowhere, I remind myself.

"How old's their sister?" I ask, wondering how she's coping with the loss of her parents and living with two brothers.

"Graduated last year. So I guess 18 or close to it," he says over the rim of his coffee cup.

Losing loved ones is never easy, but at least she's old enough to understand and has her brothers for support. Just as the thought ebbs away, I hear a loud pickup coming, and I freeze, remembering last night.

My head jerks toward the window, wondering if I should run into the back or grab a weapon.

"They're here," Fred says, setting his cup down, and my entire body relaxes, seeing a different truck pull into the parking lot.

When the driver's door opens and a hulking man steps out, my breath hitches in my throat. He has shoulder-length dark hair, tanned skin, a square jaw, and dark eyes. My heart starts hammering in my chest. He's the most gorgeous man I've ever seen.

Dang, did someone turn the heat up in here? My entire body is frozen to the spot, and sucking air into my lungs to breathe is difficult. He looks like he was carved by the gods themselves. No, my inner voice says, only the devil could create such a delicious man.

He squints his eyes, scanning the area like a hawk looking for prey. Their dark gaze holds an air of danger. That has to be Fallon, because the name suits him perfectly.

He reaches up, rubbing a hand roughly over his defined jawline, and I squeeze my thighs together while simultaneously trying to get my breathing under control. Get yourself together, I scold myself, feeling lightheaded watching him like a perv. I've never reacted to a man this way before.

"That's Fallon," Fred says, confirming what I suspected. My body tingles just hearing his name out loud while I watch him.

He begins walking around the front of the truck, and my eyes drop, seeing his massive arms and legs flex at the movement.

The passenger door opens, and an equally massive man exits. They look similar, letting me know that's his brother Duke. He looks younger by a few years, has shorter hair, and has a stare that could stop anyone in their tracks. He appears more brooding than Fallon.

But my eyes drift back to Fallon. He's like staring at a glass of water, and you're dying of thirst.

Duke turns, offering his hand up into the truck, and a small young woman exits with his help. She is beautiful but dainty. I almost laugh. Her brothers are massive mountain men, broad, muscled, and dangerous looking clad in jeans and flannel. She is barely over 5 feet in jeans and a pink blouse.

There is a slight resemblance between them, but she is so feminine and petite. She must take after their mother.

Rooted to the spot, I watch as the three of them enter the diner, ushering their sister in first. Lucy, Tom, and Doug walk out of the kitchen as if knowing they had arrived.

"Glad you're here," Tom says, sitting at a large table near the door.

My eyes stay on Fallon as he walks over to Tom, shaking his hand before greeting Doug.

I wonder what those large hands would feel like on mine?

I can't seem to take my eyes off him like a creep. His massive frame and dominating aura seem to have me captivated. Now I know why Cheryl had the reaction she did.

Any thoughts she has of jumping them for a fun night better just be for Duke, because I'll hurt her if she goes near Fallon. Crap, what's wrong with me?

The one I know is Duke scans the diner as if looking for a threat before walking over to the table where the others are sitting.

The sister has an easy smile, following Duke over to the men.

Fallon's face turns hard as he assesses Tom's face, and then his eyes go to Fred, who is still clutching his side with one hand. His expression turns deadly. "We need details this time, not cliff notes."

The deep rumble in his voice as he speaks is causing my body to malfunction.

The sister looks around with a more serious expression, shaking her head at the damage. "The Brady's are dumber than I thought. And that's saying something."

I have to hold back my laugh. I was scared at how crazy they were when they attacked us last night. But now, looking at Fallon and Duke, it's obvious that the Brady brothers are nothing compared to them.

Fallon puts his hand on his sister's back and looks down at her with soft eyes. "Why don't you get something to eat while we talk?"

Duke nods in agreement, stepping closer and placing a kiss on the top of her head before handing her some money.

She smiles at them before walking away with a "Thanks."

I sit her a menu on the bar with a smile before pulling enough coffee cups for all the men, assuming they all want coffee. While lining them all up on a tray, my crazy brain starts wondering what it would feel like to run my hands over Fallon's broad shoulders. Over the rock-hard abs, I know that shirt is concealing.

I hear chairs scraping against the floor as they all begin to sit, and I turn slightly, looking over my shoulder out of instinct.

My eyes lock with Fallon's before he drops into the seat he's holding the back of with one hand. Neither of us moves, and time seems to stop.

His mouth parts, and I swallow hard, unable to breathe as heat fills my cheeks. Heck, my whole body feels hot with him staring at me like he is.

I attempt to suck in a breath as Fallon's eyes take a slow perusal of me, leaving a trail of fire in their wake.

His eyes finally snap back up, meeting mine, and there is a definite flash of heat. He's attracted to me, too. That knowledge has my nipples hardening. Holy crap.

"Let's get them some coffee," Lucy says, jerking me out of the moment.

I nod, turning back to my task while listening to Cheryl talk to Sissy, who I now know is the name of the sister.

"Are your brothers still single?" she asks Sissy while holding up her notepad and pin.

"Why are you asking?" Sissy shoots back, dropping her menu on the bar and staring up at Cheryl with a raised brow. Her tone is no-nonsense, and I see it. She may be small, but she has the same fierce stare her brothers do.

"I'm just curious," Cheryl replies with a red face, looking nervous. I've never seen Cheryl nervous before.

"Sure you are. I'll take a cheeseburger and fries with a coke," Sissy says with the same cold stare.

Cheryl writes down the order, placing it in the window for Lucy before getting Sissy's drink. I nearly laugh out loud. Cheryl is used to getting what she wants, but not this time, it seems.

I finish pouring the last of the coffees and pick up the tray, turning to the men. What I see stops me in my tracks.

Fallon's eyes are trained on me while everyone else is talking away about last night. I get the feeling he's been watching me the whole time.

I push down the knot forming in my stomach and approach the table, placing a cup of coffee in front of each of them. When I get to the far side where Fallon is seated, he wraps an arm around my waist, jerking my body into his seated one. Thank goodness, the tray is empty now.

I gasp at the tight hold he has on me. Many customers have tried to put their hands on me since I've worked here. All of them regretted it. But this, I've never wanted anything more.

Fallon is staring at me like he wants to throw me over his shoulder and carry me off to his cave, and I'm here for it. Damn, I need to control myself.

With great effort, I suck in a breath, attempting to regain control of my aching, needy body. Big mistake. My senses are now overwhelmed with a heady masculine scent that screams, 'I am Fallon.'

My core pulses with need, and I realize just how wet my panties are.

"Be careful, Fallon," Fred says. "The last man who tried to touch Dakota without permission got a coffee pot upside the head."

Fallon's arm tightens around me, and I swear I hear him growl like a dang bear.

"And he got a warning from me. Let her go, Fallon. Dakota's a good woman, unlike the other young ones around town," Tom says, casting a quick look in Cheryl's direction.

Everyone is now staring at me, and I feel heat flood my face. I put my hand on his shoulder, pushing away from him, meeting his heated gaze. "I'm a good woman."

I repeat Tom's words, needing Fallon to know I'm not into just having a night of fun. As bad as my body craves him, I just don't think I could do that. It's not who I am.

Fallon's eyes never leave me, like he wants to undress me with them and discover all my secrets.

He runs his tongue over his bottom lip in a slow movement, and I fight the urge to press my thighs together. "I'm sure you are."

I turn, needing to get some distance between us before I combust into flames.

No one would call me a good woman if they could read my mind. Because I'm conjuring all kinds of images of what that man could do to me.

"Well, look at you," Cheryl says, laughing as I approach the counter. "You're redder than the cherry pie in the case."

"Am not. It's just hot in here," I say, putting the tray away and starting another pot of coffee.

Dang, that man has me feeling things I've never imagined. I like it, but it's a little scary too.

I no more than get the coffee perking when I turn, seeing Fallon leaning against the counter next to Sissy. His eyes are trained on me, and my panties get even wetter under his intense gaze.

"You didn't like my arm around you?" He asks, tilting his head to the side.

What the heck do I say to that? "No." I lie like a rug on the floor. It comes out without a second thought.

"Are you sure about that?" He asks with a slight smirk.

"Why?" I ask, narrowing my eyes. His cockiness seems to light a fire in me, and I'm down to wipe that smirk off his face. "You like to touch things that aren't yours?" I toss back.

His eyes flare, but his smirk grows. "What if I want to make you mine?"

Everything in me tightens at his words, and my breath becomes ragged.

"Hold up. I don't think this is a conversation a sister should be hearing," Sissy says, taking a bite of her burger but holding up her free hand.

Fallon looks down at her with a stoic expression. "You're not a child. Don't act like one."

She shoots him a look, but nothing can cover up the love they have for each other. It's obvious what a close family unit they are. Even when they're irritated with each other.

She swallows the bite after chewing before turning to face him more. "All I'm saying is if you want to talk dirty, don't do it while I'm eating. Take it outside or something."

His eyes return to me, lighting that fire inside me again. "Oh, I'd like to take the conversation somewhere, alright…" he licks his lips, letting his gaze roam my body again before locking back onto my eyes. "You got a boyfriend or husband?"

I lean back against the far wall, crossing my arms over my chest, hoping I can hide how hard my aching nipples are. "Why would I need a man?"

"Protect you. Hold you while you fall asleep at night. Make you breakfast in bed. Make you see stars while you scream his name. Should I go on?"

My heartbeat is pounding in my ears, and I'm pretty sure I'll have to throw my panties out when I get home tonight. No amount of detergent will wash away the flood of wetness he's ripped from me with his words.

"Nope, I think I've heard enough," I manage to say without sounding too affected by his words.

Sissy laughs, shoving a fry into her mouth.

"What's so funny?" he asks her with a frown.

"She's not like the other women around town chasing after you, Fallon."

I smile at that. She's beautiful and right. As bad as I want him, I'm not just looking for some quick fun or a romp. I'd regret it after, and with a man like Fallon; regrets would be painful, I have no doubt.

Fallon's eyebrows draw together, studying his sister. "What do you mean?"

Sissy takes a drink of her coke before giving him her full attention. "She's not going to go chasing after you or hang on your every word. She's the kind of woman you have to win her heart. So unless you show her you want forever, she won't give you the right now."

Holy crap, Sissy isn't just beautiful; she's smart. It's like I'm an open book, and she read me.

"Dakota doesn't date. Hell, she doesn't have fun," Cheryl says, refilling Sissy's drink. "Although, I've never seen her react to someone the way she has you."

Fallon's eyes lock onto mine again, and a slow smile spreads across his face. Dang, could he get any sexier?

"Oh yeah?" he asks.

"Ya, she thinks you're hot," Cheryl says, and I immediately want to slap her mouth closed. Permanently for embarrassing me.

"Hmm...I think she's hot, too. Very hot, in fact." His eyes stare at me like he wants to see into my soul.

Sissy groans before tossing another fry into her mouth. "I don't want to be here for this, but since I am..." she turns towards her brother again. "You're doing it all wrong. Stop acting like you just want her body and engage her mind and heart." Her tone sounds like she's scolding him, and I hold back a laugh.

The more she talks, the more I like her.

"Try harder," she says before picking up the last of her burger to finish it.

"I don't think I can get any harder," he growls under his breath, but we all hear it.

My entire body is tingling, and Sissy groans in disgust, sitting her burger down.

"You seriously just said that after what she told you?" I say in disbelief. He must think I am like the other women chasing after them. Jokes on him. I'm getting pissed now. It doesn't matter how much my body craves him.

"I did. It's true. So am I affecting you the same way?" He asks.

Yes, but I'm not admitting that.

"It's affecting me," Cheryl says, raising her hand, fanning herself as if she's about to have a heat stroke listening to our conversation.

Cheryl's beautiful and announcing her attraction to him, but his eyes never leave me. He doesn't so much as toss her a quick glance. I have his sole focus and it's not helping my body calm down.

"I told you that won't work on her. Talk to her like you care more about her as a person and not getting in her pants. Like you care about her and her future."

Fallon bends his huge frame, leaning his elbows on the counter and giving me that slow, easy smile. My legs nearly buckle at how gorgeous this mountain of a man is. "What are your dreams and wants?"

His voice is almost a growl, and my stomach clenches with want. You. That's what I want and will dream of from now on, I think, but don't say it.

"Fallon," Tom shouts from the table of men. "You want us planning this without you?"

Fallon runs his tongue over his bottom lip before he stands straight. My core is aching, but my chest tightens, knowing he's about to walk away.

"We're not done talking," he says with a smirk before returning to their table.

Can everyone in the diner hear my heart racing or see how I react to him? I hope not.

"My brother is a Neanderthal, but his heart's in the right place," Sissy says, taking a drink of her coke.

"Everything of his is in the right place," Cheryl says, watching him take his seat. It's impossible to miss the hunger in her eyes.

Sissy slams her glass down on the bar, giving her a nasty look. Cheryl's face goes red before rushing into the kitchen away from her.

"I've never seen him look at a woman the way he looks at you," Sissy says once no one's around to hear.

"Yeah?" I say, feeling my heart skip a beat at her admission. "I wasn't the one asking about him, though."

"No, you didn't. But you didn't have to. It's clear you're interested," she says, pushing her plate away.

# Chapter 4

Fallon

"Their truck is hidden in the old barn outside of town. Suggesting they took to the mountains," Tom says, looking each man in the eye sitting around the table. "They think no one will come looking for them and they can just wait it out until things cool down."

I turn to Duke, who is already staring at me, and cock a brow.

"I'm sure they're armed to the teeth by now," Fred says, and Doug agrees.

Duke rubs the scruff on his jawline as we listen to each of them talk.

"So, what were you thinking?" I ask Tom. Not that he will be handling this. I'm just curious about what's going through his head.

"We all go out to the Miller property, follow their trail up the mountain, take our money back before ending their reign of terror on all the surrounding towns."

Fred and Doug both voice their agreement while slamming their fists on the table. All three of them are getting riled up.

They don't realize that we know something they don't. Before their last arrest, a man was killed two towns over. Our cousin called us, letting us know he saw the Brady brothers leaving the scene after the man was shot, but their local sheriff wouldn't believe it. Their killers, not just thieves that enjoy terrorizing people.

They'll never stop until someone stops them permanently. And Tom, Fred, and Doug aren't the men for that job. We are.

Duke is fighting back his laughter, watching them get all worked up. I side-eye him with a stone-cold face. This isn't a time to laugh. I know what has to be done before another man dies or a woman; I think glancing back at the front of the diner.

"Wrong," Duke snarls, getting serious.

They all stop talking, turning towards him in shock.

"What's your idea?" Tom says, leaning forward in interest.

"If we all go there storming into the mountains, that's no doubt set with traps by now. People get hurt," Duke's voice is low and even.

"That's the idea. We hurt them," Fred says, fisting his hand on the table.

"Not what I meant, and you know it," Duke says, shooting him a hard look.

Time for me to set things straight. "Me and Duke go up alone. We handle them once and for all." I lay it out clear and simple. No one knows these mountains better than us.

The men all exchange looks before Tom turns an equally hard look at Duke and me. "You two are going to take care of them by yourselves?"

Fred and Doug stare at me in disbelief. They all should know better than doubting us. Our family has never let this town down in taking care of our own. We're not about to stop now.

"Yes," I deadpan.

Tom laughs, but Duke and I never crack a smile. This isn't a joking matter, and I meant every word I said.

Fred looks at Duke with a raised brow. "Is he being serious?"

Duke just stares back at him and I do smile then. "You called us to handle it, and that's what we're going to do. Take care of them."

"I called you to help, not cut us out of some retribution," Tom says, slamming his palm down on the table.

I know where he's coming from. If I were in his position, I'd want to hurt them, too, for what they did to the diner and to him. "I'll think about it."

They continue talking around me, but my eyes go to the most beautiful woman I've ever seen. Dakota is absolutely stunning. She moves around, putting gloves on before bending over with a trash can to clean up a pile of glass.

Seeing her bend over in those tight-as-hell jeans has all the air leaving my lungs. I can't look away from her slender waist and the perfect swell of that round, full ass.

It's close to noon now, and the sun beating in through the windows has sweat appearing on the back of her neck, exposed by her hair up in that ponytail. I want to lick it off. Hell, I want to lick her everywhere.

Her long black ponytail sways each time she reaches for another piece of glass, and I wonder what it would be like to have it wrapped around my fist as I plunge into her tight little body.

If her honey-brown eyes would look at me pleading as she screamed my name in pleasure while I thrust into her? She's hypnotizing to watch, and I can't tear my eyes away from her.

She stands before going over to another pile of glass with large pieces before squatting down again. When she leans forward, pushing that sweet little ass out again, a low feral growl rumbles out of me. The perfect curve of her hips is screaming for me to grab them. To take her and make her mine.

My length hardens painfully against the restriction of my jeans as images of what she would look like if I ripped her clothes to shreds and slid my fingers between her thighs. To feel her soft, wet lips and tight little hole.

Shit, this woman is mine. Not for a night, not for a few months. Eternity.

I want her to be my wife, bear my children, and be my everything. She's the one.

"So we all go scout the area to pick up their trail. Then we split up to corner them, leaving them no escape route," Tom says, jerking me out of my head.

"We'll make them pay," Fred says, slamming his hand on the table.

They can talk all they want, but that's not happening.

I stand and walk straight to my woman. She may not know it yet, but that's what she'll be.

I kneel beside her, helping her pick up the larger pieces. I see her holding back a smile, and my eyes stay focused on her lips. So pink, full, and sweet. My dick begins to throb with need, sending a jolt straight to my balls.

"Did you come over to help me or stare at me?" She asks with a full smile that has my heart slamming inside my chest. Damn, she's even more beautiful when she smiles.

"I'm here for you, Sparrow. Whatever you need," I say, watching her. I don't miss the flash of shock at my nickname for her. People only move to a town in the middle of nowhere for two reasons. They're hiding or running. Either way, my Sparrow won't be going anywhere now that she's in my sights.

"And if I tell you to leave me alone?" She cocks a challenging brow.

"Never. You're not getting rid of me." I return her challenging gaze with one of my own.

"So you'll stalk me now?" she asks with a half-grin, as if some part of her likes the idea.

"You can call me your admirer, protector, obsessive stalker, boyfriend, or future husband. Any of those are fine." My eyes stay locked on her, now shocked ones as wide as saucers.

Dakota finally snaps her gaping mouth closed before shaking her head. When she reaches for another piece of glass, I take her hand in mine, rubbing the back of it with my thumb.

With my index finger resting against her wrist, I can feel her pulse racing. My sister is right. She may be attracted to me, too, but she needs to know I'm serious. I want more than what's between her legs. I want the whole package and I'll show her somehow.

We stare into each other's eyes for several minutes before her little pink tongue comes out, wetting her lips. I follow the action with my eyes, wanting nothing more than to jerk her into my arms and taste her. But I need to control myself and not scare her off.

Dakota pulls her hand out of mine before continuing to clean up the glass. "It may sound silly to you, but this place, this town, is my first true home. Seeing it like this is heartbreaking."

I feel anger bubble up inside me. This is the first place she's felt at home. So Tom and Lucy are who she considers family, and the fucking Brady's did something to upset her. They will pay.

"I must sound pathetic, huh?" she says, shaking her head.

My chest aches to see her like this. I never want to see her upset or hurt again. This woman is so perfect. The obsession to own and claim every part of her as mine is animalistic. She's awakened the beast inside me, and there's no putting it back in its cage now.

She deserves to be taken care of, cherished, and loved. Not to be working in a run-down diner surrounded by horny truck drivers and travelers every day. I want to throw her over my shoulder, take her on my mountain, and lock her up so she's safe and loved. Where only my eyes can see her. Only my hands can touch her.

Do it...A dark voice roars in my head. My palms begin to itch thinking about someone else touching her. Tom said, customers have put their hands on my Sparrow before. I'll be damned if they do again. She's mine. I'll fucking rip their hands off if they even try to again.

"Does Sissy and Duke live with you?" she asks, getting me out of my kidnapping thoughts.

I begin helping her clean up the glass again before answering. "We all live on the Denton Mountain, but Duke and I have separate houses. Sissy stays with him in our parent's old house."

"It must be hard only having each other now," she says with sadness in her eyes.

"At first, it was after losing them. But we've always been close, so we helped each other through it." I say. All kids lose their parents at some point, but knowing that doesn't make it easy.

"I can understand that," she says, but I see a deeper sadness behind those honey-brown eyes. I want to ask about it but decide now's not the time. Soon though.

"It was hardest on Sissy. I think it still is. She and Mom were close. Now there's only us guys, so she misses the girl talk, I think."

Dakota tosses the last large piece of glass into the trash from this pile before staring into my eyes. "I can understand that. It's nice to have another woman to talk to sometimes. Even if you're talking about nothing important."

Damn, I want to cup her face and tell her how amazing she is. How so very different from other women around here are. That I would love for her and Sissy to spend time together. But I push it all down deep for now. Don't scare her, I remind myself.

The intense feelings consuming me are hard to control. But I know I have to for right now.

Mom and Dad always said my emotions drove my actions out of all their kids. Sometimes, it's made me act recklessly, but I always get the job done. I may be impulsive and hot-headed, but I'm also passionate, loyal, and fiercely protective of what's mine. And this Sparrow is mine.

Dakota goes to stand, but I'm faster, taking her hand and standing with her. My massive frame towers over hers as she looks up at me with so much desire in her eyes it nearly takes my breath away.

Now that I'm this close to her, I take my time absorbing every detail. Then I see it, and my heart stops.

It was covered with makeup until she started sweating and wiping her face with her hand.

I take her chin between my fingers, rougher than intended, turning her head to the side so I can see her face better.

Dakota lets out a little moan that would have my dick throbbing before, but now all I feel is murderous. "Who?" I ask, trying to hold back the growl. The beast she awoke in me wants blood. Rage, red-hot rage, has every muscle in my body coiling tight.

My mouth is dry, and the blood in my veins feels hot as fire. I need to hunt down whoever did this and rip them apart. Someone dared to touch what's mine!

She might think that I'm some dominant asshole, but I don't give two shits. She will know every part of me. That includes the protective, possessive, dominant primal beast that has claimed her. I will seek and destroy anything that harms her.

Dakota's eyes meet mine with concern and embarrassment. She has nothing to be embarrassed about. I fist my free hand at my side.

"Who was it?" I ask again.

"Last night. I was here, and one of the Brady brothers hit me when I tried to protect Tom," she says. Her eyes start filling with tears, like she's remembering what happened all over again.

"You were working?" I ask, trying to make sense of what she saying while my stomach coils into a tight knot. My woman was here, and she was struck.

I'd planned on ending the Brady's before they hurt or killed someone else before. But now...Now they'll bleed before I send them to hell for touching my Sparrow.

I force myself to take a calming breath and lose my hold on her chin. "Which one hit you?" The words come out slow and deliberate as I attempt to cool my temper, at least for now.

Dakota chews on her bottom lip, and she looks in deep thought. "I've never met them before, so I don't know their names. But he was bigger than the other one. Older too. But the third one yelled from the door that it was time to go. I never saw him."

I nod in understanding. There are three of them, but I know exactly who she's talking about. Only one of the brothers is big. He's the eldest and all mine when I get my hands on him.

I release her and step back, ready to leave and take care of this.

Dakota reaches out, grasping my forearm. "What are you doing, Fallon?" Her voice has a hint of worry.

Doesn't she know she never has to worry about me?

My eyes flick to our sister before landing back on Dakota. "Can you hang out with Sissy? Maybe take her to your house, and we'll pick her up tonight?" I ask, but I already know the answer.

"Of course. But tell me what you're doing." She says with wide eyes.

"To handle things." I give her hand a squeeze before storming away, heading straight for the door.

As I pass the table of men, I shoot my brother a hard look. "Time to go."

Duke knows better than to say anything or question me when I'm this pissed. I give him the same courtesy when he's mad. He sets his coffee down and follows me out to the truck.

I fire the engine up just as Duke is shutting his door.

"We have to be responsible now and be around to look after Sissy," he says, buckling his seat belt.

"I know that. Need to clear my head, scout the area, and get our game plan ready." I want to add that I have more than Sissy to look out for now. We have two women in the Denton family to care for and protect. But I save that for later.

Forty-five minutes later, we are at the old Miller place. I park, and we walk the rest of the way to the barn, staying in the tree line for coverage. I doubt they're close, but they're probably high in the mountains by now. But we need to be sure.

We approach with caution until Duke breaks the silence again. "I mean it, Fallon. We can't protect her dead. We need to plan."

I pause my steps and give him a hard look. My little brother knows exactly how to push my buttons. "The only people dying are the Brady's for touching what's mine. Now shut up, verify their trucks in the barn while I track what direction they went. Meet back here in ten minutes."

Duke's eyes flash with recognition of me calling Dakota mine. When I turned to leave, I could see him staring at us. He didn't miss our interaction. Just like I'm sure he saw the bruise on her face too. His expression goes hard and cold before giving me a chin lift.

We both go in our separate directions.

Ten minutes later, I'm back in the same spot, knowing where they went, and Duke's back a minute later.

"Trucks where Fred said it was," he growls.

I jerk my head towards the mountain. "They headed south up towards the old Crawley hunting cabin. My best guess is that's where they'll hold up."

He nods, staring in that direction. "We can't let Tom, Fred, and Doug near the front when we pin them down inside it. They'll end up shot, or worse."

I fist my hands, knowing he's right. "They can set a perimeter while we breach it. Quiet while they sleep."

Duke's eyes meet mine, and an agreement passes between us. We'll need firepower to pull this off. And they won't be expecting to be attacked in the middle of the night. We'll have the upper hand.

I grit my teeth, thinking about Dakota's face, then the fact they killed a man before flashes in my mind. They could have killed her before I even met her. "Johnny's mine."

Duke gives me a look of understanding before we turn, heading back to our pickup.

The entire way back, I keep a white-knuckle grip on the steering wheel. As bad as I want to end the Brady brothers for what they've done, today isn't the day.

Planning and firepower is the way to go so we don't get injured in the process.

I reach under the seat, pulling out the Glock I keep there. Steering with my thigh, I eject the clip, checking it's fully loaded, before popping it back in and tucking it into my waist.

"You packing now?" Duke says without looking in my direction.

"Smart thing to do under the circumstances. You should, too."

He nods, popping the glove compartment open and taking his out. It's better to be prepared than regretful, Dad always said.

# Chapter 5

Dakota

"What are you going to do now that you've graduated?" I ask Sissy as I pull the third batch of cookies out of the oven. We've finished dinner and discovered we both like to bake when we're anxious.

"I'm trying to talk my brothers into letting me go to college."

I set the hot cookie sheet down on the stove, slip off my mitt, and turn to her. She's sitting at my small kitchen table, dipping a cooled cookie into her glass of milk with a sad expression.

"What do you want to be?" I ask, curious but really wanting to know why they don't want her to get a higher education.

Sissy looks up at me with a sparkle in her eyes. "I love animals. I've always wanted to be a Veterinarian."

The joy she exudes from just speaking about it warms my chest. "Your brothers don't want you to leave?"

Sissy shakes her head. "They're protective. They'd rather me stay on the mountain forever, where they can keep me safe. But I'm wearing them down."

That sparkle in her eyes turns mischievous, and I chuckle. "I bet you are. Want to watch some TV?"

"Sure," she says, walking the few steps into my small living room.

I turn off the oven, then place the cookies into a large cookie jar before joining her.

I stifle a laugh when I see her stop flipping channels when she gets to the Discovery channel to watch big cats in the wild. But if I'm being honest, I love watching animal shows, too.

"The more time we spend together, the more I see we have in common," I say with a grin, tucking my feet up under myself, getting comfortable.

She sighs, pulling her feet up onto the couch. "It's so nice having another woman to talk to and hang out with again."

We watch TV and talk about baking, animals, and our favorite books for hours. Then, I start asking questions about her brothers and the mountain.

She is vague at first until she turns sideways, facing me fully. "You don't have to beat around the bush with me, you know," she says with a raised brow and a smile.

"What do you mean?" I ask through a laugh.

"If you want to know about my brother, just ask. You don't have to pretend you're not interested in him with me. I saw the way you two looked at each other."

There's no hiding the blush creeping onto my face. It feels like it's on fire. "I didn't specifically..."

"Look, I've got two eyes. A grown woman with a fully functioning libido. It's clear you two are into each other. So ask away." Sissy's expression is a knowing one, but her tone is no nonsense.

I feel like she is reading me again, like an open book. Like she can see straight into my soul where I keep my deepest secrets. I don't want to lie to her, so I take a deep breath, trying to gather my words.

"He's really into you," she says, tilting her head to the side, watching me.

"You think so?" I can't imagine him wanting anything more than the other men I've run across do. A fun romp in bed. I'm a former runaway, now a waitress who struggles to take care of herself every day. It's not like I have a lot to offer except for...well, me.

Sissy cocks a brow, staring at me, and my pulse pounds in my ears. "I know my brothers better than they know themselves sometimes. And Fallon has it bad when it comes to you. His eyes were glued to you all day."

My face must be as red as a tomato by now because it's on fire. "We shouldn't be talking about him like this. You're his sister."

"Do you know how many women in this town have tried to date him and Duke?" She asks with an eye roll. "It's pathetic. But they get nowhere."

"They don't date?" I ask, not being able to help myself. They're both handsome. But Fallon is gorgeous.

"They've never chased women. Our parents told us that when you meet the one, it's like being struck by lightning. You know. And you don't let that person get away." Sissy has a sparkle in her eye again and a playful smile.

My stomach does flip-flops just thinking about what she's implying. Could he possibly think I might be the one? Could he be the one for me? Would it really work out for us like it did for their parents or for Tom and Lucy?

"My brothers are wild and crazy, but they're loyal and protective. Good men, as my mother used to say," she says before turning back to the TV.

I turn, watching it, too, with a million thoughts going through my head and a smile on my face.

We watch TV in comfortable silence for another hour before Sissy speaks again. "After our parents died in the fire, I was devastated. I had nightmares and cried all the time. My brothers spent a solid week sleeping at night on each side of me. Holding me to chase the dreams away, and told me we were a family now. And we would always take care of each other. We've done that ever since."

By the time she's finished, I feel a tear run down my face. She reaches over, wiping it away. "Don't be sad. I have the best brothers in the world. And you...you have a good man that wants you. Be happy."

I smile, not sure what to say. "It's just that what you said was both so sad and so beautiful at the same time. I've never had anyone who loved and cared for me that way."

"Oh, that's about to change soon," she says with another mischievous grin.

"Whatever happens between Fallon and me, just know that I really like hanging out with you. I'm looking forward to us becoming friends," I tell her, meaning every word. I'm older than her, but life has a way of making you grow up fast. Wise beyond your years is what Lucy calls me. I think Sissy losing so much has made her the same way.

"Deal," she says, holding up her hand with her pink outstretched.

I laugh at how silly it all is with a pinky swear, but I don't hesitate to hook mine with hers. "Deal."

It's late when I look over, seeing Sissy sound asleep, curled up on the end of the couch. A soft knock on the door startles me a bit, but I scramble up to answer it.

I flip the lock, opening it with my heart pounding in my chest to see Fallon and Duke standing in the hallway.

Fallon has his arm braced on the wall and a smile on his face that has my stomach tightening. Dang, I'm definitely going to have to throw these panties out.

His eyes rake over me in a slow perusal, making a shiver go up my spine. When his eyes finally meet mine again, the heat I see in his makes my legs want to buckle. Fallon is mouthwatering, even more so with his messed hair that looks like he's been running his hands through it.

"Sorry it's so late," he says in his deep baritone voice that has my lady parts screaming; who gives a crap about the time?

We stand there for, I don't know how long, staring into each other's eyes. It's like time has stopped, and the surrounding air is crackling with sexual tension. Until I realize I must look like an idiot standing here holding the door.

"Come in," I say, backing away from the door.

Fallon stands to his full, glorious height with hunger in his eyes and walks towards me like a hunter approaching his prey.

Goosebumps rise up on my arms, and my breathing quickens with every step he takes.

I stop backing up when I feel the end of the couch hit the back of my legs, and Fallon stops a foot in front of me. He's a mountain of a man compared to me. The top of my head comes to his chest, making me have to tilt my head back to look up at him.

"Sissy fell asleep a while ago," I say, trying to get ahold of myself.

Duke walks over to where she's lying and wakes her with ease. "Come on Sissy. Time to go home." He's so gentle and carrying with her for such a large man. I'm in awe.

She groans, then stands without protest. With a quick glance at me, she smiles. "See ya later, Dakota."

"See ya, Sissy."

The relationship these three siblings share amazes me. Sissy is sweet and caring. Duke is the silent, brooding one with a hidden soft side, and Fallon... He's my wet dream come to life.

He turns his head, taking in my small apartment. "Nice," he says.

"There's not much to it," I reply. And there isn't. An open area with a small living room, kitchen, and table. The two doors off the living room area. One is for a bedroom, and other is for the bathroom. That's it.

I'm not embarrassed about it. I work hard to take care of myself, and this is what I can afford. My apartment may be small, but it's clean, and it's mine.

Fallon looks over at Duke and Sissy standing in the open doorway before looking back at me with longing. "Thanks for hanging out with Sissy."

"Don't thank me. I enjoyed her company and can't wait to hang out again."

Fallon gets that hungry look in his eyes, and my panties are getting wetter by the minute. This man controls my body and hasn't even touched me. Yet, my inner voice says, hopefully.

Fallon closes the distance between us and strokes the side of my face with the bruise. "We'll get them, and no one will hurt you again."

His voice is almost a growl, and a shudder runs through me. Fallon doesn't miss it, and he cups my face with both hands as his eyes flash dangerously.

I raise my hands, holding onto his forearms for support, because my legs are about to give out from the intense stare he's giving me. "I'm just glad you're here."

I don't know where the words came from. They just left my mouth. Honest and true.

Fallon traces his thumb over my cheek, down to my bottom lip. His eyes follow the movement with a hungry gaze. The sexual tension is a live wire that's charging the room. He feels it, too.

His tongue comes out, wetting his lips before he turns to his brother and sister. "Go on home. I'm going to stay a bit."

Duke gives him a nod, and Sissy gives us a broad smile before following her brother out, shutting the door.

My heart is pounding so hard you'd think I'd run a marathon when Fallon looks back down at me. His flannel shirt has the top two buttons undone, revealing a hint of dark hair on his chest.

It makes me wonder where it leads to. Does his abs have that same dusting of dark hair?

This man is beyond sexy with those dark eyes that look at me like he wants to devour me whole.

Don't get your hopes up just yet, I scold myself. You don't know what he wants from you in the long run. Heck, you don't even know what he wants right now, for sure.

"We baked cookies. Want some with milk?" I ask lamely, hoping it will start a conversation. Heck, anything to cool down this sexual firestorm brewing between us a little.

"That sounds good. I'm always up for baked goods," he says with a smirk, sitting down at my little wooden table, watching me.

"It's something Sissy and I have in common. We like to bake when we're stressed," I admit, getting glasses, milk, and the cookie jar and setting everything on the table.

When I pull my chair out to sit, Fallon grabs it, scooting it right beside him with that heated look again. "I want you close."

My breath catches for a minute at his words, but I simply nod and sit. Our thighs are touching, he has our chairs so close. Butterflies are doing a full workout routine in my stomach, but I love it.

He fills our glasses with milk, then takes a cookie, dipping it before holding it up to my mouth. "Open."

It's the most erotic word anyone has spoken to me. This gorgeous man wants to feed me. Yup, I open my mouth but never take my eyes off of his.

Fallon stares at my mouth, watching me take a bite. A low rumble comes from his chest when I take the bite, and his eyes flash. In a sudden movement, he has me out of my chair and onto his lap. I'm sideways, and his arms are around my waist like bands of steel.

He drops his head to my neck, inhaling me with a groan. I reach up, threading my fingers into the back of his hair as another shiver runs up my spine. I'm unsure what to do, so I just melt into him, enjoying the moment of being in his arms. The heat radiating off his massive body soaks into mine, mixed with his warm breath skating across my neck.

My body is lighting up like the Fourth of July, and I give into the feeling, if only for a few moments.

Fallon raises his head, staring into my eyes. We're so close our breaths are mingling, and I see just how hot and intense this man is up close.

I could get lost in those dark orbs of his for hours. Everything about Fallon screams sex, dominance, and possessiveness; I will set you ablaze if you let me. And boy do I want to let him. But I don't want any regrets later, I remind myself.

With a shuddering breath, I brace my hands on his shoulders and stand. He releases my waist, and I take my seat again next to him.

We sit and talk for hours. He tells me about his businesses and the mountain. How he built a home for himself and his future family after his parent's deaths. How he wants a strong unbreakable relationship like they had...and my heart starts doing a happy dance inside my chest.

I can't stop the smile that seems to have permanently set up camp on my face when he talks to me. Maybe we could have a future together.

With that thought, I open up to Fallon about growing up with two alcoholic, abusive parents and running away at sixteen years old. I've never told anyone my whole story before now. How I've taken care of myself since I was old enough to do so and been on my own.

He holds my hand, stroking it with his thumb the entire time I talk, and listens to every word without judgment. Everything seems so right and easy with him sitting here. Like we've known each other forever.

Everything about Fallon is drawing me in deeper. I just pray I don't get hurt in the process. The intense way he looks at me and touches me is both enticing and scary. As if he wants to own or possess every part of me.

"It's late. You don't want me walking up the mountain after dark, do you?" His eyes sparkle, and his voice holds a teasing tone.

"I wouldn't want you to have to hurt a bear or something on the way," I say with a playful tone and laugh. There's no doubt in my mind this man could handle anything that mountain or the animals that inhabit it could throw at him. "You can take the couch."

He turns, eyeing the couch in the living room, then cocks a brow at me in question. It's clear he is too large for it, but I'm not one of the women in town who just jumps into bed with men for fun. I've never slept with a man before. Heck, I've never done anything before.

"You want me to sleep there?"

"You didn't listen to your sister at the diner when she told you I wasn't like the women you're used to." My tone is harsher than I intended, but he needs to know that I don't just sleep around. "I've never even been on a date, for peat's sake."

As soon as those last words fly out of my mouth, I immediately want to take them back.

Fallon's eyes go wide at the admission before he nods. "Ok," he says, standing and taking my hand. His large hand engulfs my smaller one, pulling me up to stand in front of him.

With his free one, he brushes a loose tendril of hair away from my face. "We'll go at your pace."

He licks his bottom lip, staring down at me with that same hungry stare that has my panties soaked every time. It's a stare that's full of desire and want. "I'll wait until you're ready. But Dakota, don't make me wait long. It's torture not being able to touch you."

My pulse pounds in my ears when he leans down, brushing his full lips over mine in a chased kiss. "Goodnight, Sparrow."

"Goodnight, Fallon," I breathe out before gathering him a pillow and blanket from my room. He stands at the end of the couch, watching me place them down for him.

His eyes don't leave me until I'm in my room, shutting the door with a soft click. I curse myself the entire time I change my clothes and get under the covers. My body is aching for his touch.

It seems like forever before I'm able to drift off to sleep.

# Chapter 6

Dakota

I try to scream, but nothing comes out as the Brady brother leans over me holding a knife. Some part of my mind knows it's a nightmare and not real. I just have to get out of it.

I attempt screaming again, and I jolt awake with a start. My body flies up into a sitting position in the bed, and my chest heaves.

I clutch the blanket in my fists while I glance around my bedroom. It's still dark out, with only the light from the moon casting a soft glow through the window. With great effort, I take a few breaths, calming myself.

A tear slides down my cheek, and I swallow a sob at the memory of his malicious face in my dream. "It was just a nightmare," I whisper to myself.

I wipe my face and heave a sigh, relaxing my tense muscles.

Then I remember that Fallon's sleeping in the next room. The thought of him being close is what snaps me out of it.

To my shock, my bedroom door opens, and Fallon's massive frame fills the doorway. "Dakota, is everything okay?"

I clear my throat, hoping my voice doesn't crack. "Yes, I just had a nightmare."

He stands there for a few minutes staring at me, and I notice what he's wearing...Next to nothing.

He's standing with a large hand on the doorframe in just a pair of tight briefs that are doing nothing to hide what can only be described as an anaconda inside them. His thick muscular thighs beneath them are as big as tree trunks, and my mouth goes dry at the sight.

The low light from the kitchen I left on casts a soft glow behind his ripped, hard body. My eyes rake over every impressive inch of him, lingering on his abs. Then I get stuck on his broad, powerful chest before taking his arms. Holy crap...I swallow hard.

I feel like I'm parched and dying of thirst when I look lower again to the dusting of dark hair below his abs that leads to a deep V that had to be carved by the gods themselves. It trails down into his briefs to the massive bulge that goes clear to his hipbone, barely contained in them. My needy core begins pulsating with a hunger so intense it contracts with an angry vengeance.

"I heard you call out. Were you crying?" he says, stepping towards the bed.

I pull the blanket closer out of instinct when it registers in my mind what I'm wearing. Just a tank top and a pair of clean panties. No one's ever seen me in this little before.

"I'm ok. It was a nightmare."

Fallon sits on the edge of the bed and runs a hand through his long hair before locking eyes with me. My eyes immediately go to his flexing biceps at the movement.

"Was it about the attack at the diner?" His voice is rough from sleep and only increases my desire for him.

"Yes," I whisper. "But I'm ok. It helped to know you were here with me."

"I am here. And I'm not going anywhere unless you tell me to."

I smile as want and need for this sexy man flood my body. My nipples are so freaking tight they feel like I could cut glass with them right now. I'm not sure I ever want him to leave, and I need to stop letting fear rule all my decisions.

"Is the couch comfortable?" I ask, hoping he wasn't miserable on it.

"It wasn't as bad as I thought it would be."

"You can sleep here," I say, pulling the blanket back beside me. I'm not sure where my sudden boldness comes from. I'm an independent, strong, opinionated woman, but with men, I just shut them down and walk away. Not with Fallon.

Fallon's eyes go to the bed next to me before locking onto mine with a raised brow. "Are you sure, Dakota? Because make no mistake, it will happen, but only when you're ready."

I take a deep breath and nod, watching him.

He gets a serious expression, and his voice drops an octave. "Once I get my hands on you, Dakota, I won't stop until I've claimed every part of you as mine. When that happens, there's no going back. I'll never let you go. Do you understand what I'm saying?"

This incredible man wants to make me his. I've wanted him from the start. Craved his touch, but now that we've spent the night talking, getting to know one another. I want him. All of him. "Yes, I'm sure."

A slow, sexy grin spreads across his gorgeous face before he jerks the covers down further. "I'm gonna take such good care of you, Sparrow."

I move over, and he slides into bed next to me. My pulse begins to race, and nerves rack my body. When he wraps those strong arms around me, a low moan escapes as he pulls me against his massive chest. His body is radiating heat and power, setting me on fire.

Relax, don't be nervous, I chide myself. I trust this man. This big dominant alpha male that I crave more than my next breath.

He grips the back of my hair just enough to tilt my face up to his. "Give me those lips," he growls before he descends his mouth onto mine in a demanding, hungry kiss that has all the air, leaving me with a long, needy moan.

He returns it with one of his own, driving his tongue into my mouth, stroking over mine while simultaneously rocking his hips. That massive bulge grinds into my stomach, making my core clench in response as I cling to his shoulders.

Fallon pushes his massive thigh between my legs, spreading them before he shifts, coming on top of me and settling himself right where he wants to be. Right where I need him to be.

He grinds his hard length into my greedy, aching core, and I whimper at how good it feels. He smiles against my mouth before kissing me even harder.

A large, callused hand lifts the bottom of my tank before sliding over my stomach, up to my breast, where he cups it. He begins kneading and pinching my nipple, sending jolts of pleasure straight to my clit.

My moans get louder as he continues thrusting his hips forward against me, right where I need it. If he continues, I'm going to come. It's happening so fast, all the feelings and pleasure rushing through me. But I want more...I need more.

I want his hands and mouth everywhere; I need him to fill me up, making me his. To stretch and touch every part of me that's burning for him. I run my fingernails down his back, and he growls, thrusting into me harder.

My vagina is pulsing and screaming for him to take me. Make me his in every way.

"I've been hard since I first laid eyes on you. I need to sink into that tight little pussy and make it mine," he growls, alternating kissing and gentle bites along my jawline down to my neck.

The action seems to have a direct line to my greedy core by the shocks of pleasure that keeps jolting through me.

Another thrust of his hips has him hitting my clit just right, and a long moan rips from me, followed by his name. "Fallon."

I'm soaking wet, and I know he can feel it through my panties.

He dips his head lower as he pushes my shirt above my breasts. "When I saw you bend over in those tight as-hell jeans, I almost came in my pants. It was torture just watching you."

He captures a nipple in his mouth, sucking hard, and I squeal in pleasure, throwing my head back. He's like a starving man sucking it deep before flicking his tongue over my nipple.

Fallon released it with a pop, staring at the other breast with a hungry gaze. "I need you so bad, Dakota. You consume my thoughts."

He takes my other nipple into his mouth, sucking with such vigor that my walls contract, screaming for him to take me already. This is torture.

He pulls back with a feral look in his eyes. "I need to taste you, Sparrow. Right now."

His sudden movements have me releasing my grip on his back when he leans up, running his hands over my thighs while he stares at my panties.

My nipples are rock hard, begging for his attention again, but that's not where his focus is now.

I glance down at his briefs, seeing his hard shaft is now even bigger and sticking out of the top. There's pre-cum dripping from the tip, and it looks purple and angry. Oh crap, will it even fit? How big is he?

"I want to see you. All of you," I say, looking into his eyes.

"Ok," he says, resting back on his knees with a grin. "You first. Then I'll show you the last dick you'll ever see."

I want to tell him that it'll be the only one I've seen, but his hands ripping my panties off seem to have stolen any words I had prepared.

With a quick snap and tearing sound, they are flying across the room, and Fallon's eyes blaze with that feral look again as he stares down between my legs. "Fuck Dakota. You're beautiful."

My breath catches when he grabs me behind the knees, hooking them over his arms, and dives, burying his face in me. I throw my head back with a loud moan when he sucks my clit into his mouth and flicks it.

He groans and starts shaking his head from side to side like he can't get enough while the pleasure has my hips jerking off the bed. His hold on my legs tightens into a vice grip before he dips further down, pushing his tongue inside my channel. "Oh," I call out at all the intense sensations.

My orgasm is building too fast and strong, and he's not slowing down. Fallon is becoming more aggressive by the second. He goes back to my clit, flicking it so fast, and with so much pressure, I explode with a scream.

I feel him inserting a finger while he continues licking, prolonging my orgasm. Then there's another finger. He's stretching me. I'm coming down from the high twitching and shaking, and his fingers keep a slow, steady pace. Even his fingers are huge.

Fallon watches like a starving man as he pumps his fingers in and out of me, and the sensitivity is maddening. Once he pulls them out, he licks them clean before standing at the end of the bed.

Our eyes lock as he lowers his boxers, and I can't breathe at the sight when I look down. His length goes past his navel. And the girth is well...I don't think my hand will fit around it.

My eyes snap to his, and I know he can see the worry. His nostrils flare, but his voice is low, gentle. "I'll go slow, Sparrow. Make it so good for you. But you're mine now. Do you understand?"

I nod, wanting nothing more than to be his and him to be mine.

Fallon reaches down, fisting his dick and taking a few hard strokes. "You're gonna feel so good wrapped around me. Gonna fill you up, Sparrow." He licks his lips that are covered in my juices before snapping his eyes to mine.

"Anyone ever tasted my pussy before?" he growls like he's ready to start killing people.

"No," I say truthfully.

"Anyone ever taken you before?" His eyes narrow, looking even more feral.

"No."

He growls low and deep, sending a shiver through me. "Mine."

"Yes," I moan in response.

The soft glow from the moon highlights the gorgeous, sexy man staring down at me like I'm a goddess—his goddess.

I raise up enough to pull my tank over my head so we are both completely bare to each other.

Fallon's eyes roam over every inch of me from head to toe.

"You ready for me, Sparrow? Ready for me to take what's mine?"

"Yes."

"I need your words, Sparrow. Tell me."

"I'm yours, Fallon, and you're mine. Take me."

My vagina clenches with anticipation of what he's going to feel like. I know it will hurt at first. Shoot, maybe a little while. But the burning need for him outweighs any fear of pain I have.

He bends and begins crawling back up the bed. Back over on top of me. His face hovers just inches from mine, and I want him to kiss me so bad. "Touch me. Wrap your hand around me, Sparrow."

I reach between us, wrapping my hand around him the best I can, and mimic his movements, stoking him. He groans, closing his eyes. "Harder Sparrow. Grip me hard."

I do as he says and a sense of power washes over me that I'm bringing him pleasure. "I want to taste you," I say. Unsure of how much of him I can get into my mouth but I do want to try.

Fallon shakes his head no and bores his eyes into mine. "Not tonight. I need you too bad." His face looks pained, and he pulls my hand away from him. His eyes look at me with that familiar hunger as he rocks his dick through my folds and over my sensitive clit.

"Oh, Fallon," I moan out as he continues rocking his hips, coating himself with my wetness.

# Chapter 7

Fallon

My entire body is vibrating with anticipation of claiming my Sparrow. I can't believe how lucky I am that she saved herself for me.

Her sweet taste is still on my tongue, bringing out the feral beast she's awoken in me. I meant what I said...she's mine now, and I'm never letting her go.

I will own every part of her heart, body, and soul. Starting with that tight little pussy that's dripping wet just for me.

My eyes lock onto hers as I cup both sides of her face, bracing myself on my elbows. I shift my hips, notching my throbbing dick at her entrance. "You're so tight, Sparrow. But I'm going to make you feel so good once I take you."

Dakota wets her lips and clutches my shoulders before rocking her hips in rhythm with mine. My little Sparrow wants me as bad as I do her. Her mouth is open, and her eyes are full of desire. She nods, signaling she's ready.

My nostrils flare as I inhale the scent of her delicious little pussy still on my lips. The aroma sends goosebumps across my skin, and my balls tingle, knowing I'm going to be sinking inside my untouched Sparrow. Claiming her.

I ease forward, pushing the tip inside, knowing full well I'm going in bare. I'll never use a condom with her. In fact, the sooner I put a baby in that belly of hers, the better. The thought of her round and swollen with our child makes my balls ache to fill her up with my come until it's leaking down her thighs.

But most of all, to mark her with my seed as mine for eternity.

I continue pushing forward slowly as she digs her nails into me.

I slam my mouth onto hers, delving my tongue inside to taste her sweet mouth while I inch deeper into her tight channel. She's already gripping me tighter than a fist, and I'm barely inside her.

She moans, and I swallow it down like it's life. We break apart, gasping for breath, when I reach her barrier. She's so wet and tight that the beast inside me roars, wanting to slam home.

I see her face twist in pain as I nudge her hymen, so I lean down and give her a soft kiss. "You're doing so good, Sparrow. Open those beautiful eyes and look at me when I take what's mine."

She opens them with a moan, her legs, and inner walls squeezing me hard, and all I can think about is how perfect she is.

I reach a hand down between us and begin making small circles on her clit with my thumb. Her mouth falls open at the pleasure and pain combination, and she relaxes beneath me.

I bring my hips back and thrust forward, breaking through and bury myself, balls deep, bumping her womb. My Sparrow cries out as her eyes clamp closed with my dick filling her.

A single tear falls, and I kiss it away. Damn, she's so perfect. I'm going to cherish her forever.

This moment, right now...I'll never forget. It's the best moment of my life.

"I'm going to make it feel so good, Sparrow," I moan, pulling back to the tip before pushing back in slowly. I keep a slow pace until all you can hear is our moans of ecstasy filling the room.

Dakota fists my hair and starts meeting each of my thrusts, and I know she's ready for more. I hook an arm under her leg, pull it up, and begin drilling into her.

At this angle, I'm deeper, tapping her womb every time I thrust forward. That's where it needs to be while I unload. My seed needs to be in her womb.

"You're mine, Sparrow, and I'm yours," I growl as the headboard slams into the wall. That and the sound of our bodies slapping together is all that can be heard above our moans. "Your mine now... your body, mind, heart, soul, fuck every hole...It all belongs to me."

I'm slamming into her with each word to punctuate my meaning loud and clear.

"Yours, Mine," she manages to get out as I drill into her. Those sweet breasts are bouncing with each powerful thrust of my hips.

I dip my head, capturing a hard peak into my mouth while my shaft is being squeezed by her walls. She whimpers when I suck hard, bring it firmly to the roof of my mouth before sucking gently and flicking it with my tongue.

I release it, staring at them, bouncing. "So fucking perfect," I say, thrusting harder. A part of me knows I should be tender with her for the first time, but I can't. I have to pound into her, mold her to be mine and what I'm going to be giving her the rest of her life.

I look down, seeing my thick shaft going in and out of her, and an image of her stomach round with my child growing inside her womb flashes in my mind. A need...a hunger like I've never known takes over, and I know I have to breed her. The beast in me is going crazy to pound into her until I unload into her womb.

Dakota begins screaming my name, and her body convulses with the force of her orgasm. Her tight little pussy clamps down on me so hard my balls draw up tight, threatening to unload.

She's pulling my hair out by the roots as her body arches and violently trembles beneath me and I never miss a stroke. My legs shake, and I grip her tighter when my balls seize up. A jolt of pleasure shoots up my spine, and that's it.

I thrust deep, burying my full length against her cervix with a roar as I come harder than I ever have. "Dakota!" her name rips from me in a guttural voice that doesn't sound like my own as I unload my seed into her womb.

As jet after jet shoots out of me, I feel like my soul is leaving with it. She's mine forever. I've marked and claimed her.

My body continues jerking and twitching as I look down into her pleasure-filled eyes. My Sparrow looks satisfied and well-pleasured, just as I'll always make sure she is.

I pull her into my arms, rolling so she's cradled to my chest, where she will be every night from now on. Within minutes, her breathing is evened out, and I know she's drifting off.

I kiss the top of her head, inhaling a deep vanilla scent that must be her shampoo. "Sleep Sparrow. I've got you."

I close my eyes, knowing damn well I'll always take care of my Sparrow.

# Chapter 8

Dakota

A smile is permanently plastered on my face this morning during the drive to the diner. After waking up in Fallon's arms, he kissed my closed eyelids to wake me. Then he carried me into the shower, lathering every inch of my body...washing me so tenderly before rinsing me off.

His gentleness and care are in complete contrast to the gruffness he shows everyone else. Fallon squeezes my thigh with his free hand, and I side-eye him, seeing a grin on his face, but he never takes his eyes off the road.

"I better not catch another man touching you. Scratch that...I better not catch another man looking at you."

I feel heat rushing to my cheeks, and I turn, looking at him. His hair is still damp from our shower together, and he has day-old scruff on his chiseled jawline. The same jeans and flannel shirt from yesterday are stretched tight over his bulging muscles and defined chest.

"I've worked at the diner for six months, and everyone who comes through here knows better than to touch me." I pause, recalling Tom telling him about the coffee pot incident. "As far as looking at me, I can't control that."

Fallon pulls into the parking lot, shutting off the engine before he shifts, facing me. He takes my chin between his thumb and forefinger, holding me in place. The look he gives me is full of ownership. "I don't like you working where a bunch of men are. I don't like others looking at what's mine." His voice is low, bordering on a growl.

"Are you that jealous, Fallon?"

"You're mine, Sparrow. If another man gets any ideas, I'll rip him limb from limb. Understand?"

A shiver goes up my spine, and my nipples pebble. Do I understand? Heck, ya, I do. And I'm all in with this mountain man. "Yes. But you don't have to worry. I'm not interested in anyone but you."

Fallon's eyes get darker, more intense, and his nostrils flare. "Oh, I'm not worried, Sparrow. Just remember, you're mine, and I don't fucking share."

I nod, swallowing hard at the intensity of his gaze on me.

Fallon leans down, brushing his lips over mine in a soft, sweet kiss. He doesn't seem to realize that I've never been so drawn to someone. This obsessed, dominating man can command my body, my mind, and I'm scared to admit my heart. The last thought is terrifying.

I'm falling for him hard. He's saying all the right things, but some small part of me is afraid it's not real. I'm dreaming or imagining it, and I'll wake up to find it was all a figment of my imagination.

Fallon's fingers trace my cheek, and his eyes soften, following the movement.

Well, crap, I'm kidding myself. I'm already in love with this man. My pulse picks up at the admission, and a slow smile spreads on his face. Looks like his sister isn't the only person who can read people.

"I'm yours if you want me, Fallon," I say, leaning forward. The admission is a scary one, but it seems to fuel him.

He threads his fingers into my hair, staring into my eyes like he dares me to take the words back or even try to move. "And I'm yours."

His lips crash into mine in a frenzy. Lips, tongues, and teeth all clash together with such ferocity that all the air leaves me as I cling to his shoulders, trying to keep up with his movements.

"Fallon!" Duke's booming voice breaks us apart.

He slowly releases me, taking my hand, and we exit the truck, seeing Duke walking back inside the diner to where Tom, Fred, Doug, and Lucy are sitting at the large table near the back.

Fallon leads me through the diner with a stoic face still holding my hand. He pauses in the center of the room, kissing my cheek before whispering, "We'll talk more later."

His warm breath fans over my skin, causing goose bumps to rise.

Dang, this man is everything, I think as he steps back, then strides over to the table, joining them. Maybe I don't have anything to worry about. He seems as crazy about me as I am about him.

When I pry my eyes away from him, I see everyone at the table staring at me with shock and curiosity. My face immediately feels hot, and I know I'm red as a tomato again.

I turn, walking towards the back to wash my hands and put my apron on, seeing Cheryl leaning against the counter. "Hey Cheryl," I say, walking past.

"Lucky bitch," she says with a broad smile. I don't miss the jealousy in her tone.

"Yep," I reply with a grin, pushing the swinging door open. I am a very lucky woman.

When I exit the kitchen, tying my apron on, Cheryl is still in the same spot with a smirk on her face. The mischievous sparkle in her eye says she isn't going to let this go. "Spill the deets." She raises a brow at me, waiting.

"Nope." I pop the P with finality. What happened between Fallon and me is ours. I won't be sharing that with anyone.

"Seriously?" she says, in a high-pitched tone, following me around as I check each station and make sure both pots of coffee are ready to go.

"Seriously," I say, deadpan. My eyes drift to Fallon, seeing him sitting at the center of the long table with everyone else around him talking. He's such a dominating presence, even in a room full of men. He knows he has a commanding alpha presence and uses it.

The bell chimes above the door, and I swivel, seeing Sissy coming in with a smile. "Hey, Dakota."

She takes a seat at the counter, and I give her a menu. She must have been at one of the nearby shops when we arrived. "An interesting thing happened last night," she says, holding the menu but never raising her head to look at me.

"Oh ya, what's that?" I ask.

"Yep, Fallon didn't make it home last night." She gets a slow smile as her eyes slowly lift, meeting mine.

I can't hide my grin, no matter how hard I try.

"Hmmm, that's odd," I say, my cheeks heating up. "Is that unusual?" I try to play coy, but I doubt anything gets past her.

Sissy tilts her head to the side, studying me. "Do you think I'm stupid?" The words aren't harsh but more playful or teasing.

"No, just figured you'd be happy." I raise a brow, trying to do anything to hide my embarrassment that everyone realizes he spent the night at my place.

"Oh, I am. He looks happy, and so do you." She looks back at the menu before ordering a full breakfast with orange juice.

Instead of placing the ticket in the window, I go into the kitchen and begin cooking. I'm not as fast as Tom or Lucy, but I'm a good cook. More than what I can say for Cheryl. That woman should never be allowed near a kitchen. I'll trust her to get Sissy's drink and keep her company until I'm finished.

By the time I had everything plated and carried out, I saw several guys tearing down the plywood we had over the busted windows, ready to put in new glass.

My eyes go to the counter on instinct, finally noticing the new cash register and other items that were busted, now replaced. Good, I can't wait until all signs of what happened are gone.

I scan the room, appreciating all the work we put in yesterday, cleaning up the glass, and putting everything back in its place. Three women can accomplish a lot in a day.

A man enters wearing a utility belt carrying a ladder, making the bell chime above the door. He doesn't take a second to look around or say a word. His eyes go to the ceiling, spotting the bullet hole, and sets the ladder up under it.

Whoever he is, he's determined to go straight to work.

I begin wiping the counter down near Sissy, but my eyes keep going to Fallon. He, however, keeps looking from the man on the ladder filling in the hole to me. His eyes are narrowed as if he's just waiting to see if the man looks in my direction.

I almost laugh, but then a wave of jealousy hits me, thinking of another woman eyeing my man. My man, because that's what he is to me. Anger rises, and now I realize how he feels.

When he looks back at me, I raise two fingers, touch my lips, remember his lips on mine, and smile. I see Fallon's eyes darken from across the room when he realizes what I'm thinking of. I smile and wink at him.

A slow smile spreads on his face, but the look in his eyes says I will pay later for teasing him when we're alone. Thank goodness I'm behind the counter, so he can't see me squeezing my thighs together at the thought. I can't wait.

My cheeks heat up again, and I need some fresh air. I turn and walk through the kitchen out the back door. Once outside, I take a deep breath, lean against the building, and close my eyes.

I hear the door open and close behind me before I hear Cheryl's voice. "Are you alright, Dakota?"

I turn, seeing her concerned expression. "Ya, I'm good. Just needed some air for a minute."

Her eyes roam my face as if to make sure I really am before stopping on the side of my face. It's still bruised, but the green and yellow are easier to cover up with makeup than the dark blue. "It looks much better today."

She's right, it does. Covered with makeup, and the fact the swelling is almost gone makes it barely noticeable. "Thanks," I say with a sigh, leaning back against the building again. "I'm ok. It could have been much worse."

She goes back inside, passing Fallon as she does. Cheryl gives him a crooked grin before squeezing by him.

As soon as he steps in front of me, his towering frame and warm, caring eyes immediately heat up my body again. I came out here to cool off and get myself under control, and here he is, lighting me up again.

"You're not trying to run away from me, are you?" His low, dangerous tone has my body shuddering.

"Didn't even cross my mind," I say with a grin. My body is getting hotter, and my panties wetter by the second at his close proximity. I can feel the heat radiating off of him; he's so close.

Fallon takes another step, pressing his enormous body against mine, his hands on each side of my head on the wall, caging me in.

He lowers his face so his nose is nearly touching mine. "Good, because I would hunt you down and remind you where you belong, Sparrow."

Oh crap, the thought of him doing that has my core aching with need. "Just needed some air," I say. My voice is so breathy there's no way he missed it.

"Are you feeling sick?" he asks, bringing a hand to stroke my cheek, but he has a half-smile. What's that about?

"No, I feel fine." Just horny, I think, but don't say that out loud.

"Well, if you do, don't worry; it's perfectly normal." Fallon leans down, kissing my nose before giving me a loving look.

My eyebrows draw together, trying to figure out what the hell he's talking about. He leans down again and gives me a slow, passionate kiss, stroking his tongue over mine in a slow caress before pulling back.

Then it hits me. He thinks I could be pregnant. We didn't use protection...could I be?

Anything's possible, but there is no way symptoms present themselves this soon. But the look in his eyes is hopeful. He wants me pregnant.

The knowledge slams into me. But I'm not upset. In fact, butterflies erupt in my stomach and I smile without thinking. What the hell...I want this, too. I want a family with this man.

# Chapter 9

Fallon

Two days fly by as we gather more intel on the Brady brothers. We have some guys from our lumber yard who are excellent trackers taking care of the legwork. One is sitting on the barn they have their truck stashed in. Three others are mapping out the mountain to the cabin I know they're holding up in for any booby traps.

I've spent my every waking moment these past days with Dakota. She's the woman for me, and I know it. No one has ever made me feel the things she has. She owns me, body and soul.

The icing on the cake is that my sister and brother like her, too. Sissy is very vocal about it. On the other hand, Duke never says it, but his expression and hidden smiles when she's around tells me all I need to know. He approves. Not that I need his approval. I claimed her, and nothing's changing that.

It's almost closing time at the diner, and I watch my woman flutter around stocking and cleaning. Every time she looks my way, my dick twitches, wanting to sink into her.

This amazing woman has no idea what she does to me. I take another drink of coffee, never taking my eyes off her. I can't. Anytime we're in the same room, I have to watch her when my hands aren't on her. It's getting harder by the day not to throw her over my shoulder and march up the mountain like a fucking caveman.

I love her and intend to make her my wife. I may not have said the words yet, but I will.

She puts a tray of clean coffee mugs under the counter and looks around with a smile. Damn, she's beautiful. When she reaches back, untying her apron, I know she's finished for the night, and I stand ready to get her out of here.

I meet her step for step as she walks around the counter and pull her into my arms rougher than intended. But the wait to touch her while she worked has been torture.

My mouth descends on hers in a demanding kiss as I lift her off her feet. Once we're both out of breath, I sit her down before cupping her face. My Sparrow's eyes are dazed with lust, and my dick jerks seeing how she responds to me. "I love you."

Dakota's eyes go wide, and her mouth opens and closes a few times before I see tears fill her eyes. She clutches my shirt in both fists, and her breathing picks up. "I love you too, Fallon. So much it scares me."

Damn, this woman is everything. "I'll cherish you every day, Sparrow. I swear it."

A single tear falls, and I lean down, kissing it away before pulling her into my arms again. I'll give her anything, be her everything. She's mine.

My phone rings, and I reluctantly release her, pulling it from my pocket. I see Sam's name flash on the screen, and I smirk, knowing what this means, as I hit the answer button.

My eyes meet Dakota's as I talk. "Tell me what I want to hear."

"They're inside for the night, all three. Come up the south side of the mountain; it's all clear." I nod, not caring that he can't see me.

"Three a.m.," I say before hitting the end call button. Any weapons will be useless while they sleep. Even if one stays awake guarding while the other two sleep, he wouldn't be any match for me and Duke.

He'll all three aren't a match for us. But I want this quick and easy, silent, if at all possible.

Dakota gets a worried expression as I put my phone away. "Fallon, I don't want you to go. Now that I have you, I don't want to lose you," she says, gripping the front of my shirt again.

I cup her face, forcing her to look into my eyes. "You're not losing me, Sparrow. I'll handle this once and for all. Be back before you know it."

"Swear it," she chokes out.

"I'll never lie to you, Sparrow. I swear." I take her mouth in mine. The kiss is slow and sweet. A promise of our future together.

But first, I have to end these assholes before someone else gets hurt or dead because of them. They've been violent bastards just like their daddy since they could walk. Their biggest mistake was fucking with my town...touching my woman. No one gets away with that.

A tear rolls down her cheek as I pull her hands from my shirt. "Let's get you home safe."

I turn, seeing Duke's hard expression as he ushers Sissy toward the door. He is as ready to deal with the Brady brothers as I am. It's time we send another loud and clear message that nobody fucks with what's ours. This town and everything in it falls under that.

While he gets Sissy up on the mountain, I take my woman home to spend a few hours with her. Hopefully, wear her out good and proper so she sleeps before I have to leave.

# Chapter 10

Fallon

It's 2:45 a.m. and Duke just parked the truck a mile down from the old barn the Brady's have their truck stashed in. We know our man Paul is waiting for us two miles up the south pass, so Duke and I ease out of the truck, tuck our weapons at our backs, and take off at a steady jog, keeping our eyes peeled.

Once we reach him and even our breaths, I notice his expression. It's solemn. "What?" I ask through clenched teeth.

Paul shakes his head before meeting my eyes. "Got word from my cousin who is a nurse over at Mercy..." he says, and I know what he's about to say won't be good. "After the Brady's hit the diner, they hit a convenience store over in Billings. The clerk died from complications a few hours ago."

Duke growls in anger next to me, and I clench my fist. That makes two lives that we know of they've taken. Besides the fact they touched what's mine. No way they make it out of that cabin alive. "We end them tonight."

I look from Paul to Duke, and they both nod in agreement.

My hand goes back, withdrawing my gun as I stand straighter to my full height. I stare up at the face of the mountain with determination. "We go in silent and surround the cabin. Duke and I will take point on entry."

It's best that way. We both know the layout well. One open space for the living and kitchen area. There are two bedrooms to the right, and the outhouse is out back. So three rooms, and three men. No doubt one is in the main room on the couch. We'll take him first.

I see Duke sliding his hunting knife out of its sheath with a grin I know all too well. He's ready to shed blood. I nod to him, and the three of us begin our journey up.

Duke never speaks unless he has something to say, which is rare. Now's no different. There are no words for what we're about to do. I justify it as not only justice but preventing further deaths.

The family's lives that the Brady's have altered irrevocably by taking a loved one can grieve in peace, knowing they can never harm another...because we sent their killers to hell where they belong.

Once we reach the small clearing where the old Crawley hunting cabin sits, everything is quiet. I lower myself to a squatting position and give out a low bird call.

When it's returned by our other two men, I know they're in position. I glance at Paul and point for him to circle around the side while Duke goes to the back door. I'll be going through the front.

Duke's strides around the cabin are sure and steady, as if he owns the place. I'm more careful where I step, know which boards on the small front porch creak under weight.

One glance through the window tells me I was right. The embers from the fireplace illuminate the seating area, revealing a sleeping Brady. The youngest. Figures the two eldest would stick him on the couch.

It makes no difference to me.

With my left hand, I ease my knife out of my boot and slip it between the door and jam, hearing a slight click as I pry the catch back. This place never had good locks put installed.

I open the door just enough to step inside, staying to the left over the rugs as I make quick strides to the first Brady.

Movement from my peripheral lets me know that Duke is in and going to the back bedroom. Good, that means two of them will be down within minutes.

Just as I reach the couch, Jacob, the youngest, snaps his eyes open and pulls a gun from under the pillow. Before he can aim, I put a bullet between his eyes and one in the chest.

In three long strides, I have my back against the wall next to the first bedroom door, waiting for it to open. The Brady's have always run towards trouble, not away from it. So I don't worry, he'll go for the window running.

When I hear the floorboard creak, I grin. Guess they don't know this cabin as well as we do. I look down, watching the door handle, and sure enough, it's slowly turning.

If he thinks I'll wait for him to jerk it open, he's dumber than I thought. I pivot my foot, leaning out, and fire three shots. Two through the door and one to the right. Odds are, I hit him with one.

A loud thump followed by a groan tells me I was right. Duke's immediately at the other side of the door, gun drawn at the ready.

I nod in question towards the other room and he smirks. Good, that means this is the last asshole. I take a long step back before raising my leg and kicking the door open.

What greets me brings all my rage back to the surface. The man who put his hands on my woman is dragging himself towards the gun he dropped when I shot him. The man I would bet money on that was the triggerman in the other two deaths.

Everyone in three counties knows just how crazy the eldest Brady is. But he's met his match tonight. I rush forward, kicking his jaw, and his head goes back with a curse. "Sending you to hell right where you belong." Those are the last words he hears before Duke and I each put a bullet in him.

Part of me knows this was vengeance and the other part justice. No matter what it was, they'll never hurt anyone else. Good riddance.

I turn, walking back outside to see our men from the lumber yard waiting. Paul has a gas can at his feet and a lighter in his hand. I don't bother asking who thought to bring it. I'm only glad they did.

With a nod in thanks, Duke and I begin our track back down the mountain, knowing our men will handle the cleanup. Burn everything to the ground...and we'll never speak of tonight again. It's how things work on the mountain when we have to handle justice our way.

Once we reach the truck, I finally take a long look at Duke. He still has that same twisted smirk on his face as when he first walked around the cabin at the beginning of this. He enjoys it.

For me, it's something that has to be done in order to protect our town and its people. I compartmentalize it and put it away. For Duke, I'm not sure. He's a good man and would never hurt anyone that didn't deserve it. But a part of me knows he has a dark side. One that enjoys dishing out punishment and pain.

I don't ask, and he doesn't tell. We'll keep it that way.

We'll always protect what's ours. Now I have another to protect. My woman. My Sparrow.

My pulse races at the mere thought of her as I jump into the truck, slamming the door. "Let's go. Need to see my woman."

Duke tosses me a grin as he starts the engine. Just wait, I think, fastening my seatbelt. Wait until you find yours...then you'll understand.

After Duke drops me off at Dakota's place, I waste no time knocking on her door.

She swings it open in a rush like I knew she would. Looking me over for injuries wide-eyed.

I glance down, seeing a few spatters of blood on my hands and shirt.

"Not my blood," I say, stepping forward and scooping her up into my arms. With a nudge of my boot, the door shuts, and she throws her arms around my neck.

"I was worried and couldn't sleep," she says, staring at me.

I hated leaving her earlier after our argument. She wanted to go with me, but I wasn't having it. I know she's strong and would have been at my side, but she'll never be in danger again if I can help it.

I walk across the room next to the couch before reluctantly sitting her down. She trails her hands down my chest for balance, and I want them on me always.

"I need a quick shower before we talk."

Dakota's eyes bounce back and forth between mine in question, but I silence her with a finger to her full, lush lips. "You'll see when I'm done," I say before kissing her nose and walking into the bathroom.

Fifteen minutes later, I'm clean and walk out with a towel slung low on my waist, and she's on the couch. A sandwich and a glass of milk are waiting for me on the coffee table. Damn, she's going to make a perfect wife.

Not because she wants to feed me, but because she is attempting to do something thoughtful. She shows she cares in the little ways that matter, like my parents did for each other.

I sit on the couch next to her, then pull her onto my lap, straddling me. My Sparrow places her hands on my bare shoulders to brace herself, and fuck, I love this position. My mind flashes to her riding me. While I sink into that tight little body of hers.

I shake those thoughts away for now because my dick is near full mass and ready for action. But we need to talk.

I hold her hips firm against me and stare into those honey-colored eyes I love. "Make me the happiest man in the world, Sparrow. Be my wife. Marry me."

She gasps and her eyes start tearing up. I cup her face and pull her closer. "None of that, you hear me?"

She smiles and chuckles. "They're happy tears."

"Then say yes, Sparrow. Say yes right now," I growl because I need to take my woman. Need to hear her say it will be official. I want it in writing. She's mine. A ring on her finger and a baby in her belly.

"Yes!"

I inhale deep, taking in her scent, and grin. My wife. I like the sound of that. Mother of my children will be the icing on the cake.

I release her face and raise the hem of her tank top. Dakota lifts her arms, allowing me to remove it completely. My rough fingers trail over her collarbone and then circle around each taught nipple, making her throw her head back and moan.

I give each of them a pinch before I bend, sucking one into my mouth, and she rocks her hips against my hard shaft. Looks like we're getting started on those babies tonight. If I haven't already put one in her.

# Epilogue

Dakota

Three months later...

I'm carrying the last gym bag out of Duke's house toward the little single-cab pickup they bought for Sissy.

Both Fallon and Duke are hovering over her as she places a suitcase in the passenger seat. A blind man could see the frustration on her face right now. They've been arguing all morning over her going to her dorm by herself without them checking it out again.

She whirls on them with her hands on her hips, and I chuckle, approaching. She's so tiny next to these two mountain men, but no less fierce. "You went with me to scout the college. You both went with me to orientation day..." she says, pointing between them, furious. "I think I can move into the dorm by myself. So just stop."

She stomps her foot in anger and they both take a step back. I shake my head full-on, laughing now before placing the bag I carried in the back.

I pull Sissy into a hug and whisper, "You give any boys at college the same treatment if they give you a rough time." She pulls back with a wicked grin and a wink.

I walk over, wrapping my arms around my husband, the love of my life, trying to comfort him. This is hard on him and Duke both letting her go. But she's a grown woman, and it's time they treat her like it.

Fallon wraps his arms around me before dropping a hand to my stomach. I haven't started showing yet, but we've confirmed I'm pregnant. He splays his hand, covering it like it always does. Whether he hopes to feel movement, which it's too soon for, or to protect the baby, I don't know.

I do know I love it. His protectiveness and how fiercely he loves me is something I've craved my whole life. And I'll return it in spades until the day I die.

Sissy gives us all one last hug before getting in the driver's seat and rolling down the window. She looks down at Fallon's hand on my stomach before looking back up at me. "You take good care of my nephew or niece until fall break."

I laugh, leaning my back against Fallon as he holds me tighter. "Will do Sis. You go start making your dream come true," I say with a grin. She's going to make a great Veterinarian someday.

Once Sissy's truck is down the mountain and out of sight, Fallon leads me back towards our house by the hand.

"Just think, we'll be doing this again in 18 years or so," I say side-eyeing him.

Fallon stops in his tracks and gives me a scowl. "Our children aren't allowed to leave home until they're thirty. If it's a girl, maybe sixty."

I burst out laughing, knowing he's going to be crazy protective if we have a girl. I rub my belly and meet his eyes. "Our chipmunk may have something to say about that."

He shakes his head and grins. I knew I could get a smile out of him by using the nickname I'd picked for the baby. All babies have those adorable chubby cheeks I love. So chipmunk came to mind immediately when I found out we were expecting.

Fallon scoops me up bridal style, and I squeal, throwing my arms around his neck. "Let's go practice for baby number two."

I slap his hard chest, laughing. "Fallon, I haven't even had this one yet."

"That's why I said practice, Sparrow," he says, storming onto the porch before throwing the door open.

The End.

# Don't miss out!

Visit the website below and you can sign up to receive emails whenever Mel Pate publishes a new book. There's no charge and no obligation.

https://books2read.com/r/B-A-NJQEB-BUMVD

**BOOKS2READ**

Connecting independent readers to independent writers.

Did you love *CLAIMED BY FALLON (A Mountain Man Romance)*? Then you should read *Lust And Blood*[1] by Mel Pate!

My ex-military uncle raised me to be a strong and independent woman. But when an event stokes the rage I keep bottled deep inside, things get real. A single night of retribution against a deserving man puts me directly in the sights of Marco and Luca Rizzo. From there, my life turned upside down.

The Rizzo brothers are the most powerful men in the city, ruling it with an iron fist. Now, they'll do anything to make me theirs.

Beneath their expensive suits and strikingly handsome faces, they are dangerous men. Men that get what they want. Events unfold and we all reveal our true selves. All the pain and anger lying dormant comes pouring out.

In our darkest moment, can love prevail?

Lust And Blood is an 18+ MFM mafia romance with mature themes, profanity, and steam.

---

1. https://books2read.com/u/mgDj9z

2. https://books2read.com/u/mgDj9z

# Also by Mel Pate

**Firehouse 77**
The Hot Fire Chief: Firehouse 77 Book 2


**Outcasts MC**
Gia: Outcasts MC Book 1
Kane & Cowboy: Outcasts MC Book 2


**Standalone**
The Fireman Next Door: Firehouse 77 Book 1
Lust And Blood
CLAIMED BY FALLON (A Mountain Man Romance)